Elizabeth Barrett Browning

Napoleon III in Italy

And other Poems

Elizabeth Barrett Browning

Napoleon III in Italy
And other Poems

ISBN/EAN: 9783743340657

Manufactured in Europe, USA, Canada, Australia, Japa

Cover: Foto ©Andreas Hilbeck / pixelio.de

Manufactured and distributed by brebook publishing software
(www.brebook.com)

Elizabeth Barrett Browning

Napoleon III in Italy

AND OTHER POEMS.

BY

ELIZABETH BARRETT BROWNING.

PREFACE.

———◆◆◆———

THESE poems were written under the pressure of
the events they indicate, after a residence in Italy
of so many years, that the present triumph of great
principles is heightened to the writer's feelings by
the disastrous issue of the last movement, witnessed
from "Casa Guidi windows" in 1849. Yet, if the
verses should appear to English readers too pun-
gently rendered to admit of a patriotic respect to
the English sense of things, I will not excuse my-
self on such grounds, nor on the ground of my
attachment to the Italian people, and my admira-
tion of their heroic constancy and union. What I
have written has simply been written because I
love truth and justice *quand même*, "more than
Plato" and Plato's country, more than Dante and
Dante's country, more even than Shakspeare and
Shakspeare's country.

And if patriotism means the flattery of one's nation in every case, then the patriot, take it as you please, is merely a courtier, which I am not, though I have written "Napoleon III. in Italy." It is time to limit the significance of certain terms, or to enlarge the significance of certain things. Nationality is excellent in its place; and the instinct of self-love is the *root* of a man, which will develope into sacrificial virtues. But all the virtues are means and uses; and, if we hinder their tendency to growth and expansion, we both destroy them as virtues, and degrade them to that rankest species of corruption reserved for the most noble organisations. For instance, non-intervention in the affairs of neighbouring states is a high political virtue; but non-intervention does not mean, passing by on the other side when your neighbour falls among thieves,—or Phariseeism would recover it from Christianity. Freedom itself is virtue, as well as privilege; but freedom of the seas does not mean piracy, nor freedom of the land, brigandage; nor freedom of the senate, freedom to cudgel a dissident member, nor freedom of the press, freedom to calumniate and lie. So, if patriotism be a virtue indeed, it cannot mean an exclusive devotion to one's country's interest,—for that is only another form of devotion to personal interests, of family interests, or provincial interests, all of which, if not driven past themselves, are vulgar and immoral objects. Let us put away the little Pedlingtonism unworthy of a great nation, and too prevalent among us. If the man who does not look beyond this natural life is of a somewhat narrow order, what must be the man who does not look beyond his own frontier or his own sea?

I confess that I dream of the day when an English statesman shall arise with a heart too large for England, having courage, in the face of his countrymen, to assert of some suggestive policy,—"This is good for your trade; this is necessary for your domination; but it will vex a people hard by; it will hurt a people farther off; it will profit nothing to the general humanity; therefore, away with it!—it is not for you or for me." When a British minister dares to speak so, and when a

British public applauds him speaking, then shall the nation be so glorious, that her praise, instead of exploding from within, from loud civic mouths, shall come to her from without, as all worthy praise must, from the alliances she has fostered, and from the populations she has saved.

And poets, who write of the events of that time, shall not need to justify themselves in prefaces, for ever so little jarring of the national sentiment imputable to their rhymes.

ROME, *February*, 1860.

CONTENTS.

P O E M S.

NAPOLEON III. IN ITALY.

I.

EMPEROR, Emperor!
From the centre to the shore,
From the Seine back to the Rhine,
Stood eight millions up and swore
By their manhood's right divine
  So to·elect and legislate,
This man should renew the line
Broken in a strain of fate
And leagued kings at Waterloo,
When the people's hands let go.
    Emperor
    Evermore.

II.

With a universal shout
They took the old regalia out
From an open grave that day ;
From a grave that would not close,
Where the first Napoleon lay
   Expectant, in repose,
As still as Merlin, with his conquering face
Turned up in its unquenchable appeal
To men and heroes of the advancing race,
   Prepare to set the seal
Of what has been on what shall be.
     Emperor
     Evermore.

III.

The thinkers stood aside
To let the nation act.
Some hated the new-constituted fact
Of empire, as pride treading on their pride.
Some quailed, lest what was poisonous in the past
Should graft itself in that Druidic bough
   On this green now.
  Some cursed, because at last

The open heavens to which they had look'd in vain

For many a golden fall of marvellous rain

   Were closed in brass; and some

Wept on because a gone thing could not come;

And some were silent, doubting all things for

     That popular conviction,—evermore

     Emperor.

IV.

That day I did not hate

Nor doubt, nor quail, nor curse.

I, reverencing the people, did not bate

My reverence of their deed and oracle,

   Nor vainly prate

   Of better and of worse

Against the great conclusion of their will.

   And yet, O voice and verse,

Which God set in me to acclaim and sing

Conviction, exaltation, aspiration,

We gave no music to the patent thing,

Nor spared a holy rhythm to throb and swim

   About the name of him

Translated to the sphere of domination

   By democratic passion!

I was not used, at least,
Nor can be, now or then,
To stroke the ermine beast
On any kind of throne,
(Though builded by a nation for its own,)
And swell the surging choir for kings of men—
    ' Emperor
      Evermore.'

                    V.   .

But now, Napoleon, now
That, leaving far behind the purple throng
    Of vulgar monarchs, thou
    Tread'st higher in thy deed
    Than stair of throne can lead
    To help in the hour of wrong
The broken hearts of nations to be strong,—
Now, lifted as thou art
To the level of pure song,
We stand to meet thee on these Alpine snows!
And while the palpitating peaks break out
Ecstatic from somnambular repose
With answers to the presence and the shout,

We, poets of the people, who take part
With elemental justice, natural right,
   Join in our echoes also, nor refrain.
We meet thee, O Napoleon, at this height
At last, and find thee great enough to praise.
Receive the poet's chrism, which smells beyond
   The priest's, and pass thy ways ;—
An English poet warns thee to maintain
God's word, not England's :—let His truth be true
And all men liars ! with His truth respond
To all men's lie. Exalt the sword and smite
On that long anvil of the Apennine
Where Austria forged the Italian chain in view
Of seven consenting nations, sparks of fine
   Admonitory light,
Till men's eyes wink before convictions new.
Flash in God's justice to the world's amaze,
Sublime Deliverer !—after many days
Found worthy of the deed thou art come to do—
   Emperor
   Evermore.

VI.

But Italy, my Italy,
Can it last, this gleam ?
 2

Can she live and be strong,
Or is it another dream
Like the rest we have dreamed so long?
   And shall it, must it be,
That after the battle-cloud has broken
She will die off again
Like the rain,
Or like a poet's song
Sung of her, sad at the end
Because her name is Italy,—
Die and count no friend?
It is true,—may it be spoken,
That she who has lain so still,
With a wound in her breast,
And a flower in her hand,
And a grave-stone under her head,
While every nation at will
Beside her has dared to stand
And flout her with pity and scorn,
Saying, 'She is at rest,
She is fair, she is dead,
And, leaving room in her stead
To Us who are later born,
This is certainly best!'

Saying, ' Alas, she is fair,

Very fair, but dead,

And so we have room for the race.'

—Can it be true, be true,

That she lives anew ?

That she rises up at the shout of her sons,

At the trumpet of France,

And lives anew ?—is it true

That she has not moved in a trance,

As in Forty-eight ?

When her eyes were troubled with blood

Till she knew not friend from foe,

Till her hand was caught in a strait

Of her cerement and baffled so

From doing the deed she would ;

And her weak foot stumbled across

The grave of a king,

And down she dropt at heavy loss,

And we gloomily covered her face and said,

' We have dreamed the thing ;

She is not alive, but dead.'

VII.

Now, shall we say
Our Italy lives indeed?
And if it were not for the beat and bray
Of drum and trump of martial men,
Should we feel the underground heave and strain,
Where heroes left their dust as a seed
   Sure to emerge one day?
And if it were not for the rhythmic march
Of France and Piedmont's double hosts,
   Should we hear the ghosts
Thrill through ruined aisle and arch,
Throb along the frescoed wall,
Whisper an oath by that divine
They left in picture, book and stone
That Italy is not dead at all?
Ay, if it were not for the tears in our eyes
These tears of a sudden passionate joy
   Should we see her arise
From the place where the wicked are overthrown,
   Italy, Italy? loosed at length
   From the tyrant's thrall,
Pale and calm in her strength?
Pale as the silver cross of Savoy

When the hand that bears the flag is brave,
And not a breath is stirring, save
  What is blown
Over the war-trump's lip of brass,
Ere Garibaldi forces the pass !

VIII.

  Ay, it is so, even so.
  Ay, and it shall be so.
Each broken stone that long ago
She flung behind her as she went
In discouragement and bewilderment
Through the cairns of Time, and missed her way
  Between to-day and yesterday,
  Up springs a living man.
And each man stands with his face in the light
  Of his own drawn sword,
Ready to do what a hero can.
Wall to sap, or river to ford,
Cannon to front, or foe to pursue,
Still ready to do, and sworn to be true,
  As a man and a patriot can.
Piedmontese, Neapolitan,

2*   B

Lombard, Tuscan, Romagnole,
Each man's body having a soul,—
Count how many they stand,
All of them sons of the land,
Every live man there
Allied to a dead man below,
And the deadest with blood to spare
To quicken a living hand
In case it should ever be slow.
Count how many they come
To the beat of Piedmont's drum,
With faces keener and grayer
Than swords of the Austrian slayer,
All set against the foe.
 'Emperor
 Evermore.'

IX.

Out of the dust, where they ground them,
Out of the holes, where they dogged them,
Out of the hulks, where they wound them
In iron, tortured and flogged them;
Out of the streets, where they chased them,

Taxed them and then bayoneted them,—
Out of the homes, where they spied on them,
(Using their daughters and wives,)
Out of the church, where they fretted them,
Rotted their souls and debased them,
Trained them to answer with knives,
Then cursed them all at their prayers!—
Out of cold lands, not theirs,
Where they exiled them, starved them, lied on them;
Back they come like a wind, in vain
Cramped up in the hills, that roars its road
The stronger into the open plain;
Or like a fire that burns the hotter
And longer for the crust of cinder,
Serving better the ends of the potter;
Or like a restrainèd word of God,
Fulfilling itself by what seems to hinder.
'Emperor
Evermore.'

x.

Shout for France and Savoy!
Shout for the helper and doer.

Shout for the good sword's ring,
Shout for the thought still truer.
Shout for the spirits at large
Who passed for the dead this spring,
Whose living glory is sure.
Shout for France and Savoy!
Shout for the council and charge!
Shout for the head of Cavour;
And shout for the heart of a King   .
That's great with a nation's joy.
    Shout for France and Savoy!

XI.

Take up the child, Mac Mahon, though
Thy hand be red
From Magenta's dead,
And riding on, in front of the troop,
  In the dust of the whirlwind of war
Through the gate of the city of Milan, stoop
And take up the child to thy saddle-bow,
Nor fear the touch as soft as a flower
  Of his smile as clear as a star!
Thou hast a right to the child, we say,

Since the women are weeping for joy as those
Who, by thy help and from this day,
  Shall be happy mothers indeed.
They are raining flowers from terrace and roof:
  Take up the flower in the child.
While the shout goes up of a nation freed
  And heroically self-reconciled,
Till the snow on that peaked Alp aloof
Starts, as feeling God's finger anew,
And all those cold white marble fires
Of mounting saints on the Duomo-spires
  Flicker against the Blue.
    ' Emperor
    Evermore.'

                XII.

    Ay, it is He,
Who rides at the King's right hand !
Leave room to his horse and draw to the side,
Nor press too near in the ecstasy
Of a newly delivered impassioned land :
    He is moved, you see,
    He who has done it all.

They call it a cold stern face;
    But this is Italy
Who rises up to her place!—
For this he fought in his youth,
Of this he dreamed in the past;
The lines of the resolute mouth
Tremble a little at last.
Cry, he has done it all!
    'Emperor
    Evermore.'

XIII.

It is not strange that he did it,
Though the deed may seem to strain
To the wonderful, unpermitted,
For such as lead and reign.
But he is strange, this man:
The people's instinct found him
(A wind in the dark that ran
Through a chink where was no door),
And elected him and crowned him
    Emperor
    ·Evermore.

XIV.

Autocrat? let them scoff,
  Who fail to comprehend
That a ruler incarnate of
  The people, must transcend
All common king-born kings.
These subterranean springs
A sudden outlet winning,
Have special virtues to spend.
The people's blood runs through him,
Dilates from head to foot,
Creates him absolute,
And from this great beginning
Evokes a greater end
To justify and renew him—
      Emperor
      Evermore.

XV.

What! did any maintain
That God or the people (think!)
Could make a marvel in vain?—
Out of the water-jar there,
Draw wine that none could drink?

Is this a man like the rest,
This miracle, made unaware
By a rapture of popular air,
And caught to the place that was best?
You think he could barter and cheat
As vulgar diplomates use,
With the people's heart in his breast?
Prate a lie into shape
Lest truth should cumber the road;
Play at the fast and loose
Till the world is strangled with tape;
Maim the soul's complete
To fit the hole of a toad;
And filch the dogman's meat
To feed the offspring of God?

XVI.

Nay, but he, this wonder,
He cannot palter nor prate,
Though many around him and under,
With intellects trained to the curve,
Distrust him in spirit and nerve
Because his meaning is straight.

Measure him ere he depart
With those who have governed and led;
Larger so much by the heart,
Larger so much by the head.

  Emperor
  Evermore.

XVII.

He holds that, consenting or dissident,
 Nations must move with the time;
Assumes that crime with a precedent
 Doubles the guilt of the crime;
—Denies that a slaver's bond,
 Or a treaty signed by knaves,
(*Quorum magna pars* and beyond
Was one of an honest name)
Gives an inexpugnable claim
To abolishing men into slaves.

  Emperor
  Evermore.

XVIII.

He will not swagger nor boast
 Of his country's meeds, in a tone

3

Missuiting a great man most
    If such should speak of his own;
Nor will he act, on her side,
    From motives baser, indeed,
Than a man of a noble pride
    Can avow for himself at need;
Never, for lucre or laurels,
    Or custom, though such should be rife,
Adapting the smaller morals
    To measure the larger life.
He, though the merchants persuade,
    And the soldiers are eager for strife,
Finds not his country in quarrels
    Only to find her in trade,—
While still he accords her such honor
    As never to flinch for her sake
Where men put service upon her,
    Found heavy to undertake
And scarcely like to be paid:
    Believing a nation may act
    Unselfishly—shiver a lance
(As the least of her sons may, in fact)
    And not for a cause of finance.
        Emperor
        Evermore.

XIX.

Great is he,

Who uses his greatness for all.

His name shall stand perpetually

    As a name to applaud and cherish,

Not only within the civic wall

For the loyal, but also without

    For the generous and free.

    Just is he,

Who is just for the popular due

    As well as the private debt.

The praise of nations ready to perish

    Fall on him,—crown him in view

    Of tyrants caught in the net,

And statesmen dizzy with fear and doubt!

And though, because they are many,

    And he is merely one,

And nations selfish and cruel

Heap up the inquisitor's fuel

To kill the body of high intents,

And burn great deeds from their place,

Till this, the greatest of any,

May seem imperfectly done;

Courage, whoever circumvents!

Courage, courage, whoever is base!
The soul of a high intent, be it known,
Can die no more than any soul
Which God keeps by him under the throne;
And this, at whatever interim,
Shall live, and be consummated
Into the being of deeds made whole.
Courage, courage! happy is he,
Of whom (himself among the dead
And silent), this word shall be said;
—That he might have had the world with him,
But chose to side with suffering men,
And had the world against him when
He came to deliver Italy.

   Emperor
   Evermore.

THE DANCE.

I.

You remember down at Florence our Cascine,
  Where the people on the feast-days walk and drive,
And, through the trees, long-drawn in many a green
    way,
    O'er-roofing hum and murmur like a hive,
    The river and the mountains look alive?

II.

You remember the piazzone there, the stand-place
  Of carriages a-brim with Florence Beauties,
Who lean and melt to music as the band plays,
    Or smile and chat with some one who a-foot is,
    Or on horseback, in observance of male duties?
    3*

III.

'Tis so pretty, in the afternoons of summer,
   So many gracious faces brought together!
Call it rout, or call it concert, they have come here,
   In the floating of the fan and of the feather,
   To reciprocate with beauty the fine weather.

IV.

While the flower-girls offer nosegays (because *they* too
   Go with other sweets) at every carriage-door;
Here, by shake of a white finger, signed away to
   Some next buyer, who sits buying score on score,
   Piling roses upon roses evermore.

V.

'And last season, when the French camp had its station
   In the meadow-ground, things quickened and grew
      gayer
Through the mingling of the liberating nation
   With this people; groups of Frenchmen everywhere,
   Strolling, gazing, judging lightly . . 'who was fair.'

VI.

Then the noblest lady present took upon her
  To speak nobly from her carriage for the rest;
' Pray these officers from France to do us honour
  By dancing with us straightway.'—The request
  Was gravely apprehended as addressed.

VII.

And the men of France bareheaded, bowing lowly,
  Led out each a proud signora to the space
Which the startled crowd had rounded for them—
    slowly,   •
  Just a touch of still emotion in his face,
  Not presuming, through the symbol, on the grace.

VIII.

There was silence in the people: some lips trembled,
  But none jested.   Broke the music, at a glance:
And the daughters of our princes, thus assembled,
  Stepped the measure with the gallant sons of France.
  Hush! it might have been a Mass, and not a dance.

IX.

And they danced there till the blue that overskied us
　　Swooned with passion, though the footing seemed
　　　　sedate ;
And the mountains, heaving mighty hearts beside us,
　　Sighed a rapture in a shadow, to dilate,
　　And touch the holy stone where Dante sate.

X.

Then the sons of France bareheaded, lowly bowing,
　　Led the ladies back where kinsmen of the south
Stood, received them ;—till, with burst of overflowing
　　Feeling . . . husbands, brothers, Florence's male
　　　　youth,
　　Turned, and kissed the martial strangers mouth to
　　　　mouth.

XI

And a cry went up, a cry from all that people !
　　—You have heard a people cheering, you suppose,
For the Member, mayor . . with chorus from the
　　　　steeple?

This was different : scarce as loud perhaps, (who knows ?)
For we saw wet eyes around us ere the close.

XII.

And we felt as if a nation, too long borne in
   By hard wrongers, comprehending in such attitude
That God had spoken somewhere since the morning,
   That men were somehow brothers, by no platitude,
   Cried exultant in great wonder and free gratitude.

A TALE OF VILLAFRANCA.

———◆———

I.

My little son, my Florentine,
  Sit down beside my knee,
And I will tell you why the sign
  Of joy which flushed our Italy,
Has faded since but yesternight;
And why your Florence of delight
  Is mourning as you see.

II.

A great man (who was crowned one day)
  Imagined a great Deed:
He shaped it out of cloud and clay,
  He touched it finely till the seed
Possessed the flower: from heart and brain
He fed it with large thoughts humane,
  To help a people's need.

III.

He brought it out into the sun—
   They blessed it to his face :
' O great pure Deed, that hast undone
   So many bad and base !
O generous Deed, heroic Deed,
Come forth, be perfected, succeed,
   Deliver by God's grace.

IV.

Then sovereigns, statesmen, north and south,
   Rose up in wrath and fear,
And cried, protesting by one mouth,
   ' What monster have we here ?
A great Deed at this hour of day ?
A great just Deed—and not for pay ?
   Absurd,—or insincere.

V.

' And if sincere, the heavier blow
   In that case we shall bear,
For where's our blessed ' status quo,'
   Our holy treaties, where,—

Our rights to sell a race, or buy,
Protect and pillage, occupy,
    And civilize despair?'

VI.

Some muttered that the great Deed meant
    A great pretext to sin;
And others, the pretext, so lent,
    Was heinous (to begin).
Volcanic terms of 'great' and 'just?'
Admit such tongues of flame, the crust
    Of time and law falls in.

VII.

A great Deed in this world of ours?
    Unheard of the pretence is:
It threatens plainly the great Powers;
    Is fatal in all senses.
A just deed in the world?—call out
The rifles! be not slack about
    The national defences.

VIII.

And many murmured, 'From this source
    What red blood must be poured!'
And some rejoined, ''Tis even worse;
    What red tape is ignored!'
All cursed the Doer for an evil
Called here, enlarging on the Devil,—
    There, monkeying the Lord!

IX.

Some said, it could not be explained,
    Some, could not be excused;
And others, 'Leave it unrestrained,
    Gehenna's self is loosed.'
And all cried, 'Crush it, maim it, gag it!
Set dog-toothed lies to tear it ragged,
    Truncated and traduced!'

X.

But HE stood sad before the sun,
    (The peoples felt their fate).
'The world is many,—I am one;
    My great Deed was too great.

God's fruit of justice ripens slow :
Men's souls are narrow ; let them grow.
My brothers, we must wait.'

XI.

The tale is ended, child of mine,
    Turned graver at my knee.
They say your eyes, my Florentine,
    Are English : it may be :
And yet I've marked as blue a pair
Following the doves across the square
    At Venice by the sea.

XII.

Ah, child ! ah, child ! I cannot say
    A word more.   You conceive
The reason now, why just to-day
    We see our Florence grieve.
Ah child, look up into the sky !
In this low world, where great Deeds die,
    What matter if we live ?

A COURT LADY.

I.

Her hair was tawny with gold, her eyes with purple
were dark,
Her cheeks' pale opal burnt with a red and restless
spark.

II.

Never was lady of Milan nobler in name and in race;
Never was lady of Italy fairer to see in the face.

III.

Never was lady on earth more true as woman and
wife,
Larger in judgment and instinct, prouder in manners
and life.

IV.

She stood in the early morning, and said to her maidens,
    ' Bring
That silken robe made ready to wear at the court of the
    king.

V.

· Bring me the clasps of diamond, lucid, clear of the
    mote,
Clasp me the large at the waist, and clasp me the small
    at the throat.

VI.

' Diamonds to fasten the hair, and diamonds to fasten
    the sleeves,
Laces to drop from their rays, like a powder of snow
    from the eaves.'

VII.

Gorgeous she entered the sunlight which gathered her
    up in a flame,
While, straight in her open carriage, she to the hospital
    came.

VIII.

In she went at the door, and gazing from end to end,
'Many and low are the pallets, but each is the place of
    a friend.'

IX.

Up she passed through the wards, and stood at a young
    man's bed:
Bloody the band on his brow, and livid the droop of his
    head.

X.

'Art thou a Lombard, my brother?   Happy art thou,'
    she cried,
And smiled like Italy on him: he dreamed in her face
    and died.

XI.

Pale with his passing soul, she went on still to a
    second:
He was a grave hard man, whose years by dungeons
    were reckoned.

XII.

Wounds in his body were sore, wounds in his life were
soarer.

'Art thou a Romagnole?' Her eyes drove lightnings
before her.

XIII.

Austrian and priest had joined to double and tighten the
cord .

Able to bind thee, O strong one,—free by the stroke
of a sword.

XIV.

'Now be grave for the rest of us, using the life over-
cast

To ripen our wine of the present, (too new,) in glooms
of the past.'

XV.

'Down she stepped to a pallet where lay a face like
a girl's

Young, and pathetic with dying,—a deep black hole in
the curls.

XVI.

'Art thou from Tuscany, brother? and seest thou,
    dreaming in pain,
Thy mother stand in the piazza, searching the ist of the
    slain?'

XVII.

Kind as a mother herself, she touched his cheeks with
    her hands :
'Blessed is she who has borne thee, although she should
    weep as she stands.'

XVIII.

On she passed to a Frenchman, his arm carried off by a
    ball :
Kneeling, . . 'O more than my brother! how shall I
    thank thee for all?'

XIX.

'Each of the heroes around us has fought for his land
    and line,
But *thou* hast fought for a stranger, in hate of a wrong
    not thine.

XX.

'Happy are all free peoples, too strong to be dispossessed.
But blessed are those among nations, who dare to be
 strong for the rest!'

XXI.

Ever she passed on her way, and came to a couch where
 pined
One with a face from Venetia, white with a hope out of
 mind.

XXII.

Long she stood and gazed, and twice she tried at the
 name,
But two great crystal tears were all that faltered and
 came.

XXIII.

Only a tear for Venice?—she turned as in passion and
 loss,
And stooped to his forehead and kissed it, as if she were
 kissing the cross.

XXIV.

Faint with that strain of heart she moved on then to
>   another,
Stern and strong in his death. 'And dost thou suffer,
>   my brother?'

XXV.

Holding his hands in hers:—'Out of the Piedmont
>   lion
Cometh the sweetness of freedom! sweetest to live or
>   to die on.'

XXVI.

Holding his cold rough hands—'Well, oh well have ye
>   done
In noble, noble Piedmont, who would not be noble alone.'

XXVII.

Back he fell while she spoke. She rose to her feet with
>   a spring—
'That was a Piedmontese! and this is the Court of the
>   King.'

AN AUGUST VOICE.

" Una voce augusta."—

MONITORE TOSCANO.

I.

You'll take back your Grand Duke?
  I made the treaty upon it.
Just venture a quiet rebuke;
  Dall' Ongaro write him a sonnet;
Ricasoli gently explain
  Some need of the constitution:
He'll swear to it over again,
  Providing an 'easy solution.'
You'll call back the Grand Duke.

II.

You'll take back your Grand Duke?
  I promised the Emperor Francis
To argue the case by his book,
  And ask you to meet his advances.

The Ducal cause, we know,

    (Whether you or he be the wronger)

Has very strong points;—although

    Your bayonets, there, have stronger.

You'll call back the Grand Duke.

III.

You'll take back your Grand Duke?

    He is not pure altogether.

For instance, the oath which he took

    (In the Forty-eight rough weather)

He'd ' nail your flag to his mast,'

    Then softly scuttled the boat you

Hoped to escape in at last,

    And both by a ' Proprio motu.'

You'll call back the Grand Duke.

IV.

You'll take back your Grand Duke?

    The scheme meets nothing to shock it

In this smart letter, look,

    We found in Radetsky's pocket;

Where his Highness in sprightly style
　　Of the flower of his Tuscans wrote,
‘ These heads be the hottest in file ;
　　Pray shoot them the quickest.’　Quote,
And call back the Grand Duke.

V.

You'll take back your Grand Duke ?
　　There *are* some things to object to.
He cheated, betrayed, and forsook,
　　Then called in the foe to protect you.
He taxed you for wines and for meats
　　Throughout that eight years' pastime
Of Austria's drum in your streets—
　　Of course you remember the last time
You called back your Grand Duke.

VI.

You'll take back the Grand Duke ?
　　It is not race he is poor in,
Although he never could brook
　　The patriot cousin at Turin.

His love of kin you discern,

By his hate of your flag and me—

So decidedly apt to turn

All colours at sight of the Three.*

You'll call back the Grand Duke.

VII.

You'll take back your Grand Duke?

'Twas weak that he fled from the Pitti;

But consider how little he shook

At thought of bombarding your city!

And, balancing that with this,

The Christian rule is plain for us;

. . Or the Holy Father's Swiss

Have shot his Perugians in vain for us.

You'll call back the Grand Duke.

VIII.

Pray take back your Grand Duke.

—I, too, have suffered persuasion.

All Europe, raven and rook,

Screeched at me armed for your nation.

---

* The Italian tricolor: red, green, and white.

Your cause in my heart struck spurs;
  I swept such warnings aside for you:
My very child's eyes, and Hers,
  Grew like my brother's who died for you.
You'll call back the Grand Duke?

IX.

You'll take back your Grand Duke?
  My French fought nobly with reason,—
Left many a Lombardy nook
  Red as with wine out of season.
Little we grudged what was done there,
  Paid freely your ransom of blood:
Our heroes stark in the sun there,
  We would not recall if we could.
You'll call back the Grand Duke?

X.

You'll take back your Grand Duke?
  His son rode fast as he got off
That day on the enemy's hook,
  When I had an epaulette shot off.

Though splashed (as I saw him afar, no,
   Near) by those ghastly rains,
The mark, when you've washed him in Arno,
   Will scarcely be larger than Cain's.
You'll call back the Grand Duke.

XI.

You'll take back your Grand Duke?
   'Twill be so simple, quite beautiful:
The shepherd recovers his crook,
   . . If you should be sheep, and dutiful.
I spoke a word worth chalking
   On Milan's wall—but stay,
Here's Poniatowsky talking,—
   You'll listen to *him* to-day,
And call back the Grand Duke.

XII.

You'll take back your Grand Duke?
   Observe, there's no one to force it,—
Unless the Madonna, St. Luke
   Drew for you, choose to endorse it.

I charge you by great St. Martino
 And prodigies quickened by wrong,
Remember your Dead on Ticino ;
 Be worthy, be constant, be strong.
—Bah !—call back the Grand Duke ! !

CHRISTMAS GIFTS.

ὡς βασιλει, ὡς θεω, ὡς νεκρῳ.

GREGORY NAZIANZEN.

I.

THE Pope on Christmas Day
  Sits in St. Peter's Chair ;
But the peoples murmur and say,
  ' Our souls are sick and forlorn,
And who will show us where
  Is the stable where Christ was born ?'

II.

The star is lost in the dark ;
  The manger is lost in the straw ;
The Christ cries faintly . . hark ! . .
  Through bands that swaddle and strangle—
But the Pope in the chair of awe
  Looks down the great quadrangle.

III.

The magi kneel at his foot,
   Kings of the east and west,
But, instead of the angels, (mute
   Is the ' Peace on earth' of their song,)
The peoples, perplexed and opprest,
   Are sighing, ' How long, how long ?'

IV.

And, instead of the kine, bewilder in
   Shadow of aisle and dome,
The bear who tore up the children,
   The fox who burnt up the corn,
And the wolf who suckled at Rome
   Brothers to slay and to scorn.

V.

Cardinals left and right of him,
   Worshippers round and beneath,
The silver trumpets at sight of him
   Thrill with a musical blast :
But the people say through their teeth,
   ' Trumpets? we wait for the Last !'

VI.

He sits in the place of the Lord,   •
    And asks for the gifts of the time ;
Gold, for the haft of a sword,
    To win back Romagna averse,
Incense, to sweeten a crime,
    And myrrh, to embitter a curse.

VII.

Then a king of the west said, ' Good !—
    ' I bring thee the gifts of the time ;
Red, for the patriot's blood,
    Green, for the martyr's crown,
White, for the dew and the rime,
    When the morning of God comes down.'

VIII.

    —O mystic tricolor bright !
    The Pope's heart quailed like a man's :
The cardinals froze at the sight,
    Bowing their tonsures hoary :
And the eyes in the peacock-fans
    Winked at the alien glory.

IX.

·But the peoples exclaimed in hope,
   ' Now blessed be he who has brought
These gifts of the time to the Pope,
   When our souls were sick and forlorn.
—And *here* is the star we sought,
   To show us where Christ was born!

ITALY AND THE WORLD.

I.

FLORENCE, Bologna, Parma, Modena.
　When you named them a year ago,
So many graves reserved by God, in a
　Day of judgement, you seemed to know,
To open and let out the resurrection.

II.

And meantime, (you made your reflection
　If you were English) was nought to be done
But sorting sables, in predilection
　For all those martyrs dead and gone,
Till the new earth and heaven made ready.

III.

And if your politics were not heady,
　Violent, . . 'Good,' you added, 'good

In all things! mourn on sure and steady.
　　Churchyard thistles are wholesome food
For our European wandering asses.

IV.

'The date of the resurrection passes
　　Human fore-knowledge : men unborn
Will gain by it (even in the lower classes),
　　But none of these.   It is not the morn
Because the cock of France is crowing.

V.

' Cocks crow at midnight, seldom knowing
　　Starlight from dawn-light : 'tis a mad
Poor creature.'   Here you paused, and growing
　　Scornful, . . suddenly, let us add,
The trumpet sounded, the graves were open.

VI.

Life and life and life! agrope in
　　The dusk of death, warm hands, stretched out
For swords, proved more life still to hope in,
　　Beyond and behind.   Arise with a shout,
Nation of Italy, slain and buried !

VII.

Hill to hill and turret to turret
  Flashing the tricolor,—newly created
Beautiful Italy, calm, unhurried,
  Rise heroic and renovated,
Rise to the final restitution.

VIII.

Rise; prefigure the grand solution
  Of earth's municipal, insular schisms,—
Statesmen draping self-love's conclusion
  In cheap, vernacular patriotisms,
Unable to give up Judæa for Jesus.

XI.

Bring us the higher example; release us
  Into the larger coming time:
And into Christ's broad garment piece us
  Rags of virtue as poor as crime,
National selfishness, civic vaunting.

X.

No more Jew nor Greek then,—taunting
  Nor taunted;—no more England nor France!

But one confederate brotherhood planting
 One flag only, to mark the advance,
Onward and upward, of all humanity.

XI.

For fully developed Christianity
 Is civilisation perfected.
' Measure the frontier,' shall it be said,
 ' Count the ships,' in national vanity?
—Count the nation's heart-beats sooner.

XII.

For, though behind by a cannon or schooner,
 That nation still is predominant,
Whose pulse beats quickest in zeal to oppugn or
 Succour another, in wrong or want,
Passing the frontier in love and abhorrence.

XIII.

Modena, Parma, Bologna, Florence,
 Open us out the wider way!
Dwarf in that chapel of old St. Lawrence
 Your Michel Angelo's giant Day,
With the grandeur of this Day breaking o'er us!

XIV.

Ye who, restrained as an ancient chorus,
　　Mute while the coryphæus spake,
Hush your separate voices before us,
　　Sink your separate lives for the sake
Of one sole Italy's living for ever!

XV.

Givers of coat and cloak too,—never
　　Grudging that purple of yours at the best,—
By your heroic will and endeavour
　　Each sublimely dispossessed,
That all may inherit what each surrenders!

XVI.

Earth shall bless you, O noble emenders
　　On egotist nations! Ye shall lead
The plough of the world, and sow new splendours
　　Into the furrow of things, for seed,—
Ever the richer for what ye have given.

XVII.

Lead us and teach us, till earth and heaven
　　Grow larger around us and higher above.

Our sacrament-bread has a bitter leaven;
  We bait our traps with the name of love,
Till hate itself has a kinder meaning.

XVIII.

Oh, this world: this cheating and screening
  Of cheats! this conscience for candle-wicks,
Not beacon-fires! this over-weening
  Of under-hand diplomatical tricks,
Dared for the country while scorned for the counter!

XIX.

Oh, this envy of those who mount here,
  And oh, this malice to make them trip!
Rather quenching the fire there, drying the fount here,
  To frozen body and thirsty lip,
Than leave to a neighbour their ministration.

XX.

I cry aloud in my poet-passion,
  Viewing my England o'er Alp and sea.
I loved her more in her ancient fashion:
  She carries her rifles too thick for me,
Who spares them so in the cause of a brother.

XXI.

Suspicion, panic? end this pother.
    The sword, kept sheathless at peace-time, rusts.
None fears for himself while he feels for another:
    The brave man either fights or trusts,
And wears no mail in his private chamber.

XXII.

Beautiful Italy! golden amber
    Warm with the kisses of lover and traitor!
Thou who hast drawn us on to remember,
    Draw us to hope now: let us be greater
By this new future than that old story.

XXIII.

Till truer glory replaces all glory,
    As the torch grows blind at the dawn of day;
And the nations, rising up, their sorry
    And foolish sins shall put away,
As children their toys when the teacher enters.

XXIV.

Till Love's one centre devour these centres
    Of many self-loves; and the patriot's trick
3

To better his land by egotist ventures,
   Defamed from a virtue, shall make men sick,
As the scalp at the belt of some red hero.

XXV.

For certain virtues have dropped to zero,
   Left by the sun on the mountain's dewy side ;
Churchman's charities, tender as Nero,
   Indian suttee, heathen suicide,
Service to rights divine; proved hollow :

XXVI.

And Heptarchy patriotisms must follow.
   —National voices, distinct yet dependent,
Ensphering each other, as swallow does swallow,
   With circles still widening and ever ascendant,
In multiform life to united progression,—

XXVII.

These shall remain.   And when, in the session
   Of nations, the separate language is heard,
Each shall aspire, in sublime indiscretion,
   To help with a thought or exalt with a word
Less her own than her rival's honour.

XXVIII.

Each Christian nation shall take upon her
  The law of the Christian man in vast:
The crown of the getter shall fall to the donor,
  And last shall be first while first shall be last,
And to love best shall still be, to reign unsurpassed.

A CURSE FOR A NATION.

I HEARD an angel speak last night,
    And he said, ' Write !
Write a Nation's curse for me,
And send it over the Western Sea.'

I faltered, taking up the word :
    ' Not so, my lord !
If curses must be, choose another
To send thy curse against my brother.

' For I am bound by gratitude,
    By love and blood,
To brothers of mine across the sea,
Who stretch out kindly hands to me.'

'Therefore,' the voice said, ' shalt thou write
     My curse to-night.
From the summits of love a curse is driven,
As lightning is from the tops of heaven.'

' Not so,' I answered. ' Evermore
     My heart is sore
For my own land's sins : for little feet
Of children bleeding along the street :

' For parked-up honors that gainsay
     The right of way :
For almsgiving through a door that is
Not open enough for two friends to kiss :

' For love of freedom which abates
     Beyond the Straits :
For patriot virtue starved to vice on
Self-praise, self-interest, and suspicion :

' For an oligarchic parliament,
     And bribes well-meant.
What curse to another land assign,
When heavy-souled for the sins of mine !

'Therefore,' the voice said, 'shalt thou write
          My curse to-night.
Because thou hast strength to see and hate
A foul thing done *within* thy gate.'

                                        .

' Not so,' I answered once again.
          To curse, choose men.
For I, a woman, have only known
How the heart melts and the tears run down.'

'Therefore,' the voice said, 'shalt thou write
          My curse to-night.
Some women weep and curse, I say,
(And no one marvels,) night and day.

' And thou shalt take their part to-night,
          Weep and write.
A curse from the depths of womanhood
Is very salt, and bitter, and good.'

So thus I wrote, and mourned indeed,
          What all may read.
And thus, as was enjoined on me,
I send it over the Western Sea.

THE CURSE.

I.

BECAUSE ye have broken your own chain
    With the strain
Of brave men climbing a Nation's height,
Yet thence bear down with brand and thong
On souls of others,—for this wrong
    This is the curse.   Write.

Because yourselves are standing straight
    In the state
Of Freedom's foremost acolyte,
Yet keep calm footing all the time
On writhing bond-slaves,—for this crime
    This is the curse.   Write.

Because ye prosper in God's name,
    With a claim
To honour in the old world's sight,
Yet do the fiend's work perfectly
In strangling martyrs,—for this lie
    This is the curse.   Write.

II.

Ye shall watch while kings conspire
Round the people's smouldering fire,
    And, warm for your part,
Shall never dare—O shame!
To utter the thought into flame
    Which burns at your heart.
            This is the curse.   Write.

Ye shall watch while nations strive
With the bloodhounds, die or survive,
    Drop faint from their jaws,
Or throttle them backward to death,
And only under your breath
    Shall favor the cause.
            This is the curse.   Write.

Ye shall watch while strong men draw
The nets of feudal law
    To strangle the weak,
And, counting the sin for a sin,
Your soul shall be sadder within
    Than the word ye shall speak.
            This is the curse.   Write.

When good men are praying erect
That Christ may avenge his elect
   And deliver the earth,
The prayer in your ears, said low,
Shall sound like the tramp of a foe
    That's driving you forth.
     This is the curse.   Write.

When wise men give you their praise,
They shall pause in the heat of the phrase,
   As if carried too far.
When ye boast your own charters kept true,
Ye shall blush;—for the thing which ye do
   Derides what ye are.
    This is the curse.   Write.

When fools cast taunts at your gate,
Your scorn ye shall somewhat abate
   As ye look o'er the wall,
For your conscience, tradition, and name
Explode with a deadlier blame
   Than the worst of them all.
    This is the curse.   Write.

Go, wherever ill deeds shall be done,

Go, plant your flag in the sun

   Beside the ill-doers!

And recoil from clenching the curse

Of God's witnessing Universe

   With a curse of yours.

      THIS is the curse.   Write.

New and Standard Books

PUBLISHED BY

C. S. FRANCIS AND COMPANY,

554 BROADWAY, NEW YORK.

The French Metropolis;

Paris as seen during the Spare Hours of a Medical Student. By Aug. Kinsley Gardner, M. D. Second edition, revised. $1.00.

The same work on large paper, and illustrated by twenty-five steel engravings by Heath and others. $2.00.

A New Home. Who'll Follow?

Or, Glimpses of Western Life. By Mrs. Mary Clavers (Mrs. Kirkland). Fourth edition, revised by the author, and illustrated by engravings from designs by F. O. C. Darley. $1.25. Extra gilt, $1.50.

"Incomparably the cleverest picture of western life ever sketched."

"It would be difficult to condense a greater amount and variety of real wit and sparkling humour in so small a compass, though one had a whole library to collate from."—*Tribune.*

Tour of Duty in California;

Including a Description of the Gold Region, with notices of Lower California, the Gulf, and Pacific Coasts, &c. By Joseph Warren Revere, U. S. N. With a Map and Plates, from original designs. $1.00.

"The great charm of the book is the graphic, easy, racy manner in which the style of living, habits, and customs of the people are described."—*C. Inquirer.*

Discourses on Human Nature.

Human Life, and the Nature of Religion. By Rev. Orville Dewey D. D. 1 vol. $1.00.

Discourses on the Nature of Religion,

And on Commerce and Business. By Rev. Orville Dewey, D. D. 1 vol. $1.00.

Discourses and Reviews

Upon Questions in Controversial Theology and Practical Religion. By Rev. Orville Dewey, D. D. 1 vol. $1.00.

"In rich, deep, noble thought, in apt and forcible illustration, in impressive appeals, in an earnest, manly eloquence, in a living spirit and power—power to convince the reason, to sway the affections, to move the conscience, guiding while it quickens its actions, to wake up all the slumbering energies of the soul, make it feel its responsibleness, make it feel that religion is a reality, the great, solemn, and blessed reality of its being—in all these respects we are willing to compare the twenty-four sermons of this volume (Human Life, &c.) with any similar volume given to the world from any other denomination of Christians."—*Christian Examiner.*

i

A Course of English Reading,

Adapted to every taste and capacity. By Rev. James Pycroft, B. A. Edited with Alterations, Emendations, and Additions, by J. A. Spencer, D. D. 75 cents.

The Shakspeare Gift Book.

Tales of the Girlhood of Shakspeare's Heroines. By Mary Cowden Clarke, author of the "Concordance to Shakspeare." With fine Illustrations on Steel. Cloth, $1.25; extra gilt, $1.50.

The Shakspeare Tales.

Being a Second Series of the above, by the same author; with fine Engravings. Cloth, $1.25; extra gilt, $1.50.

"Two charming Gift Books for young persons, and well suited for the reading of full grown and cultivated ladies."

The Constitutional Text Book.

Containing Selections from the Writings of Daniel Webster; The Declaration of Independence; The Constitution of the United States; and Washington's Farewell Address. With Copious Indexes. $1.25.

The Poets and Poetry of Europe.

With Biographical Notices and Translations from the earliest period to the present time. Comprising Translations from the Anglo-Saxon, Icelandic, Swedish, Dutch, German, French, Italian, Spanish, Portuguese, &c., &c. By Henry W. Longfellow. One large 8vo. volume. $5. Morocco, $7.50.

Prose Writers of Germany.

By Frederick H. Hedge. 1 vol., 8vo. With Portraits of Goethe, Luther, Lessing, Mendelssohn, Herder, Schiller, Richter, and Schlegel. Cloth, $3.00; gilt, $3.50; morocco, $5.00.

Dietetics of the Soul.

From the German of Ernest Von Feuchtersleben, M. D. 62½ cents.

"A book of deep thought to suggest thought."

"A collection of rich fragments of great practical use."

The Undying One,

Sorrows of Rosalie, and other Poems. By the Hon. Mrs. Norton Cloth, $1.00; extra, $1.50; morocco, $2.50.

Speeches of Kossuth.

Condensed and Abridged with Kossuth's express sanction. By Francis W. Newman. With Portrait. Cloth, $1.00.

"More eloquent speeches cannot be found in the English language."

Eöthen; or, Traces of Travel.

Brought Home from the East. A new Edition. 63 cents.

Geometry and Faith,

A Fragmentary Supplement to the Ninth Bridgewater Treatise By Rev. Thomas Hill. 38 cts.

'The truths of natural religion are impressed in indelible characters on every fragment of the material world."—*Babbage.*

Zenobia:

Or, The Fall of Palmyra; An Historical Romance, by William Ware. New edition, complete in one volume. With a portrait of the author. Cloth, $1.25. 1 vol. gilt, $1.50. On large superfine paper, 1 vol. 8vo. cloth, $2.00; antique or morocco, $3.50.

"An ancient classic from the pen of a modern writer. A fine specimen of that form of moral romance, of which the samples are few."—*S. Patriot.*

"One of the most brilliant additions to American literature."—*N. A. Review.*

Aurelian,

Or, Rome in the Third Century; a Sequel to Zenobia. by same author. New edition, to match Zenobia, at the same prices.

Studies in Christian Biography;

Or, Hours with Theologians and Reformers. By Rev. Samuel Osgood. 1 vol. 12mo. $1.00.

CONTENTS.—Augustine and his times; Augustine and his works; Chrysostom and the Ancient Pulpit; Jerome and his times; Jerome and his works; John Calvin and the reformed system; Teresa and the Devotees of Spain; Faustus Socinus and the revival of Unitarian Principles; Hugo Grotius and the Arminians; George Fox and the English Spiritualists; Swedenborg and the Mysticism of Science; John Wesley and Methodism; Jonathan Edwards and the new Calvinism; John Howard and Prison Reform.

"We have seldom risen from the perusal of a book which has given us more pleasure, and from which we have derived more information than this."—*Providence Journal.*

"This is the work of an accomplished scholar. The general reader will hardly appreciate the amount of learning and labour and extended literary culture which is condensed in this volume."—*Examiner.*

Thoughts on the Poets.

By Henry T. Tuckerman. Being Essays on the Lives, Characters, and Writings of the following Poets:—Petrarch, Collins, Thomson, Crabbe, Byron, Burns, Coleridge, Hemans, Drake, Goldsmith, Pope, Young, Shelley, Moore, Campbell, Keats. 75 cts.

Christian Aspects of Faith and Duty.

A volume of Sermons, by John James Tayler. With an Introduction by Rev. H. W. Bellows of New York. 1 vol. 12mo. $1.00.

"Mr. Tayler's work is alive in every sentence. It is not made up of the dust and bones of decayed dogmas and formalisms, but is fresh and full from the fountains of vital experience. It is affectionate and practical, instructive and edifying, deserving a place in every liberal Christian's library."—*Inquirer.*

Midsummer Eve;

A Fairy Tale of Love. By Mrs. S. C. Hall. Illustrated. 63 cts. Gilt extra, fine edition, 88 cts.

CHOICE POETRY.

LONGFELLOW.

The Poets and Poetry of Europe;

With Biographical Notices and Translations. From the earliest period to the present time. By Henry W. Longfellow. Comprising translations from the Anglo-Saxon, Icelandic, Swedish, Dutch, German, French, Italian, Spanish, Portuguese, &c., &c. In one large 8vo. volume of 750 pages.

"The most complete work of the kind in English literature."—*Boston Courier.*

"A more desirable work for the scholar or man of taste, has scarcely ever been issued in the United States."—*Tribune.*

NORTON.

The Dream, and Other Poems;

Including the Child of the Islands. By the Hon. Caroline Elizabeth Sarah Norton. With a fine Portrait. Cloth, $1.00: extra, $1.50; morocco, $2.50.

"The Dream is a very beautiful poem, the frame-work of which is simply a lovely mother watching over a lovely daughter asleep; which daughter dreams, and when awaked tells her dream; which dream depicts the bliss of a first love and an early union, and is followed by the mother's admonitory comment, importing the many accidents to which wedded happiness is liable, and exhorting to moderation of hope, and preparation for severe duties. It is in this latter portion of the poem that the passion and the interest assume a personal hue; and passages occur which sound like javelins hurled by an Amazon."—*Quarterly Review.*

"There can be no question that the performance (The Child of the Islands) bears throughout the stamp of extraordinary ability—the sense of easy power very rarely deserts us. But we pause on the bursts of genius; and they are many. * * * The exquisite beauty of the verses is worthy of the noble womanly feelings expressed in them. * * * We wish we had room for a score more of these masterly sketches—but we hope we have given enough to show that we have not observed with indifference this manifestation of developed skill—this fairest wreath as yet won in the service of the graver Muses for the name of SHERIDAN."—*Quarterly Review.*

"This is poetry. true poetry, and of the sort we unfeignedly approve—the genuine product of a cultivated mind, a rich fancy, and a warm, well regulated heart.'

The Undying One,

The Sorrows of Rosalie, and Miscellaneous Poems. By Hon. Mrs. Norton. A new volume, containing Poems never before published in a collected form. Cloth, $1.00; extra, $1.50.

"This lady is the Byron of our modern poetesses. She has very much of that intense personal passion by which Byron's poetry is distinguished from the larger grasp and deeper communion of Wordsworth. She has also Byron's beautiful intervals of tenderness, his strong practical thought, and his forcible expression. It is not an artificial imitation, but a natural parallel."—*Quarterly Review.*

CHOICE POETRY.

WORDSWORTH.

Poems by William Wordsworth;

With an Introductory Essay on his Life and Writings, by H. T. TUCKERMAN. Containing his most characteristic and beautiful pieces. With a portrait. Cloth, 75 cents. Gilt, $1.

"Wordsworth's poetry stands distinct in the world. That which to other men is an occasional pleasure, or possibly delight, and to other poets an occasional transport, *the seeing this visible Universe*, is to him, a Life—one Individual Human Life—namely, his Own, travelling the whole journey from the cradle to the grave. And that Life—for what else could he do with it?—he has verified—sung. And there is no other such song."—CHRISTOPHER NORTH, *in Blackwood.*

The Excursion:

A Poem, by William Wordsworth. Complete in one vol. 75 cents. Gilt, $1.

"The noblest poem in the English language, since Milton's Paradise Lost."—R. H. DANA.

"The influence of the genius of Wordsworth, in correcting the poetic taste of the age by weaning it from the pompous inanities that marked the close of the last century, and enlisting the sympathies, feelings, and taste in favor of nature, and that kindly philanthropy which does honor to human nature, has been immense. While the influence of nature upon man was his theme, he was frequently as just as profound.

"The 'Excursion,' by far the noblest production of the author, was first printed in 1814, and contains passages of sentiment, description, and pure eloquence, not excelled by any living poet. The principal character is a poor Scottish pedlar, who traverses the mountains in company with the poet, and is made to discourse with profound philosophy of the beauty and grandeur of nature. The edition of Messrs. Francis & Co., is a very beautiful one."—*Democratic Review.*

COLERIDGE.

The Poems of Samuel Taylor Coleridge.

Complete in one volume. With an Introductory Essay on his Life and Writings, by H. T. TUCKERMAN. Beautifully printed, $1.

"A mine of thought, feeling, and poesy, in a small space. The world has learned to appreciate the wonderful genius of Coleridge; and it is no more necessary now to defend and to praise his effusions, than those of Milton or Shakspeare."

SCOTT.

Waverley Poetry:

Being the Poems scattered through the Waverley Novels, attributed to anonymous sources, but presumed to be written by SIR WALTER SCOTT. With Titles and Index. 1 vol. 12mo. 75 cents.

CHOICE POETRY

The Poems of Elizabeth Barrett Browning.

A new edition, corrected by the last London edition, revised and partly re-written by the author. In two volumes. $2.25

"Mrs. Browning is, in our judgment, the first poet of her sex—the Milton among women."—*Christian Inquirer.*

"The richest and most powerful poetry which has come to us in these recent years from the female mind."—*Independent.*

"If this lady is not a great poet, who is?"—*Fraser's Magazine.*

"Mrs. Browning is entitled to dispute with Tennyson the honor of being the greatest living poet of England. Certainly, no woman of that country has yet equalled her in poetry. Her best poems, both in spirit and execution, are in the highest rank of art."—*Illustrated News.*

"That Miss Barrett has done more, in poetry, than any woman, living or dead, will scarcely be questioned; that she has surpassed all her poetical cotemporaries of either sex (with a single exception) is our deliberate opinion—not idly entertained, we think, nor founded on any visionary basis. Her poetic inspiration is the highest—we can conceive nothing more august."—*E. A. Poe.*

"Mrs. Browning's poems are marked by strength of passion, by intensity of emotion, and by high religious aims, sustained and carried out by an extraordinary vigor of imagination and felicity of expression. * * * The hopefulness of the poetry—the religious hopefulness which rises with prophetic power over tombs and deserts—is what commends it to us most, brought out as it is in all the parts with an imagination so strong, and in tones so beautiful. It is pleasant to find a writer of such unquestioned ability as Mrs. Browning, and with a love of nature so pure and hearty, turning away from the pantheistic tendencies of the age, and from the exclusive love and worship of nature, to recognize in simplicity of soul the graces and sanctities of a Christian faith, and to dwell amid the beloved and hallowed scenes which a Christian heart and imagination can create around us."—*Christian Register.*

Prometheus Bound, and other Poems;

including Sonnets from the Portuguese, Casa Guidi Windows, etc. By ELIZABETH BARRETT BROWNING. 75 cents.

Elizabeth Barrett Browning is undoubtedly the most spiritual and vigorous female writer of poetry of the age. She is at once a thorough scholar and a true woman, and writes from genuine sentiment and high aspiration. Those who have not learned to appreciate her lofty and touching verses, have a great pleasure in store. To such as know her, we need not commend any thing from her pen. We cannot, however, forbear saying that a peculiar interest invests the present volume. After Miss Barrett married Robert Browning—a man of peculiar and exquisite genius—they went to Italy. From her windows in Florence she had glimpses of the late struggle for liberty, and these induced her to think and feel on the subject; the result is before us. In addition, we have all her poems not included in the other two volumes, and a series of sonnets—the best in the English language, since Wordsworth's last, and full of intellect, sensibility, and grace."—*Home Journal.*

"This is *the* poetical offering of the year. The author, next to Tennyson, claims a hearing on the ground of that inherent right possessed by all men and women of genius. Miss Barrett has learning, (her Æschylus is a very different gentleman from the old prosing of other translators,) thought, profound feeling, artistic skill. The subject of the last poem, CASA GUIDI WINDOWS, is Italy and the recent struggles for liberty, and in it Mrs. Browning, in her peculiar manner of fervid inspiration and artistic carelessness, pours out her soul on the theme which of all within the scope of human thought is the most exciting to a true poet."

PUBLISHED BY C. S. FRANCIS & CO., NEW YORK.

Prose Writers of Germany.

BY FREDERICK H. HEDGE, D. D.

Illustrated with an engraved Title-page from a design by Leutze; and portraits of Goethe, Luther, Lessing, Mendelssohn, Herder, Schiller, Richter, and Schlegel. Complete in one volume octavo.

Cloth, $3.00; gilt, $3.50; antique morocco, $5.00.

Contents.

LUTHER,	HAMANN,	GOETHE,	ZSCHOKKE,
BOEHME,	WIELAND,	SCHILLER,	F. SCHLEGEL,
SANCTA CLARA,	MUSAUS,	FICHTE,	HARDENBERG,
MOSER,	CLAUDIUS,	RICHTER,	TIECK,
KANT,	LAVATER,	A. W. SCHLEGEL,	SCHELLING,
LESSING,	JACOBI,	SCHLEIERMACHER,	HOFFMANN,
MENDELSSOHN,	HERDER,	HEGEL,	CHAMISSO.

This work comprises a list of the most eminent writers of Germany, together with copious extracts from their works, beginning with LUTHER and reaching up to the present time. For those who are interested in the literature of Germany, it presents a valuable aid in becoming more intimately acquainted with the German mind: and to the curious an excitement which will grow stronger as their taste is cultivated.

We find here valuable extracts, given from their prose writings. Although the writers follow in chronological order, and LUTHER stands at the head of his intellectual brethren, the longest space is allowed to those who claim our greatest attention; and GOETHE therefore occupies the most conspicuous position both in the specimens given and the selection of the pieces. Next to GOETHE, SCHILLER appears in an article upon Naïve and Sentimental Poetry. Then we have LESSING, the first critic of his time. Next to him comes HERDER, a devout philosopher, and a clear-sighted intellect.. The two brothers SCHLEGEL—William, the noble interpreter and translator of Shakspeare, and Frederic, known best by his investigations of the language and wisdom of the Indians— follow him, and MOSES MENDELSSOHN, a Jewish philosopher, closes the series of these writers.

"The author of this work—for it is well entitled to the name of an original production, though mainly consisting of translations—Rev. Dr. Hedge, of Providence, is qualified. as few men are in this country, or wherever the English language is written, for the successful accomplishment of the great literary enterprise to which he has devoted his leisure for several years."

"We venture to say that there cannot be crowded into the same compass a more faithful representation of the German mind, or a richer exhibition of the profound thought, subtle speculation, massive learning and genial temper, that characterize the most eminent literary men of that nation."—*Harbinger*.

"What excellent matter we here have. The choicest gems of exuberant fancy the most polished productions of scholarship, the richest flow of the heart, the deepest lessons of wisdom, all translated so well by Mr. Hedge and his friends, that they seem to have been first written by masters of the English tongue."

"We have read the book with rare pleasure, and have derived not less information than enjoyment."—*Knickerbocker*.

WRITINGS OF L. MARIA CHILD.

Philothea;
A Grecian Romance. Third edition. 75 cts.

"Every page of it breathes the inspiration of genius, and shows a highly culti vated taste in literature and art."—*N. A. Review.*

Letters from New York.
Seventh edition. 2 vols. $1.50.

"I cordially thank the public for the hearty welcome they have given this unpretending volume. I rejoice in it as a new proof that whatsoever is simple, sincere, and earnest, will find its way to the hearts of men."—*Preface.*

The Mother's Book.
Eighth edition. 62 cts.

"For sound moral instruction and practical good sense, we know of no work of its class worthy to be compared to it."—*N. Y. Tribune.*

Biographies of Good Wives.
Third edition. 75 cts.

"We commend this pleasing collection to all those women who are ambitious, like its subjects, to become good wives."—*S. Patriot.*

History of the Condition of Women
In various Ages and Nations. 2 vols. Fifth edition. $1.25.

"Information as to the past and present condition of one-half the human race, put together in that lively and attractive form which is sure to grow up beneath the hand of Mrs. Child."

Flowers for Children.
A Series of volumes in Prose and Verse, for Children of various ages. 37 cts. each. In one volume, 88 cts.

"A collection of gems in which sparkle all the beauties of truth, holiness, and love, to attract the mind of youth in its first unfoldings."

Fact and Fiction.
A collection of Stories. 75 cts.

"There is a fresh and loveable heartiness in this book—there is music in it—it is full of humanity, and benevolence, and noble affection. It is the free, unrestrained outpourings of the enlightened heart of a poet, an artist, and a woman."—*Tribune.*

Memoirs of Madame De Stael,
And of Madame Roland. A new edition, revised and enlarged. 75 cts.

The Progress of Religious Ideas,
Through Successive Ages. 3 vols. 12mo. $4.

"My motive for writing has been a very simple one; I wished to show that *theology* is not *religion*, with the hope that I might help to break down partition walls; to ameliorate what the eloquent Bushnell calls '*baptized* hatreds' of the human race.' * * * Those who wish to obtain candid information, without caring whether it does or does not sustain any favourite theory of their own may perhaps thank me for saving them the trouble of searching through large and learned volumes; and if they complain of want of profoundness, they may be willing to accept simplicity and clearness in exchange for depth."

Progress of Religious Ideas

THROUGH SUCCESSIVE AGES. By L. MARIA CHILD. 3 vols. royal 12mo. $4.00.

> God sends his teachers unto every age,
> To every clime, and every race of men,
> With revelations fitted to their growth
> And shape of mind, nor gives the realm of TRUTH
> Into the selfish rule of one sole race ;
> Therefore, each form of worship that hath swayed
> The life of man, and given it to grasp
> The master-key of knowledge, REVERENCE,
> Unfolds some germs of goodness and of right.
>
> J. R. LOWELL.

These handsome volumes contain a historical review of the religious ideas which have been current in different nations, and in successive ages of the world. The religions of Hindostan, Egypt, China, Tartary, Chaldea, Persia, Greece, and Rome, the Celts and Jews, are surveyed in the first volume. The second treats of the Jewish religion after their exile, takes a retrospect of preceding ages, and gives the writer's view of Christianity in the first and second centuries. The Christian religion and Mohammedanism are the principal themes of the third volume. The style of the work is familiar, simple, and beautiful.

CONTENTS.

Priesthood; Idolatry; Times of the Judges; Samuel; David; Th
Temple; Solomon; Kingdoms of Israel and Judah; Book of the Law
The Kings after Solomon; Exile to Babylon.

VOL. II. *Jews after the Exile*—Chaldean Schools; Daniel in Persia
Cyrus the Great; Samaritans; Rebuilding the Temple; Ezra's Laws
Priests and Levites; The Sabbath; Festivals; Fasts; Prophets; An
gels; Events in Jewish History; Sects; Oral Law; John the Baptist
Jesus; Messiah; Sacred Books; Talmud; Solomon's Wisdom; Im
portance of Jewish Records as viewed by themselves and by others
Destruction of Jerusalem; Modern Jews. *Retrospective View*—Com
parison between Hindoos and Hebrews; One God; The Second God
Communication between Hebrews and Persians; Ideas of God; Name
of God; The Trinity; The Word; Intermediate Spirits, in descending
series; Transmigration; Incarnations; The Golden Age, past and
future; Messiahs; Immortality; Atonement; Evil Spirits; Miracles
Oracles, and Prophecies; Inspiration; Animal Magnetism; Publi
Doctrines and Secret Doctrines; Light and Truth; Immodest Symbols
No Religion Monotheistic; Theocracies; Martyrdom. *Christianity*—
Days of the Apostles; Enmity of the Jews; Roman Persecution unde
Nero; Traditions concerning the Apostles; Miracles by Vespasian
Philo, Apollonius, Simon Magus, Cerinthus; Persecution under Tragan
and succeeding emperors; Martyrdom; Early Christian Fathers; Opin
ions and Customs of the Early Fathers; Church Government and Dis
cipline; Celibacy; Sunday; Festivals; Celsus; Judaism; Benevo
lence of Christians; The Earliest Sects; Gnostics; New Platonists.

VOL. III. *Christianity*—Constantine; Virgil's Fourth Eclogue; Chris
tian Sects; Constantius; Julian; Jovian; Valentinian; Theodosius
the Great; The Later Christian Fathers; their opinions and customs
extracts from their writings; Festivals and Fasts; Bishops; Councils
Hermits and Monks; Monasteries; Nuns; Gentiles or Pagans; Jews
Samaritans; Heretics; Gregory the Great; Slavery; Churches, Images
Saints, and Rosaries; Christian Sacred Books; Spurious Books; Na
tions converted to Christianity; Separate Churches. *Mohammedanism*
—Mohammedan Sacred Books. *Concluding Chapter. List of Book:
consulted.*

NOTICES OF THE PRESS.

"No true scholar, who has himself faithfully worked over the remains of
antiquity, can fail to follow its pages with perpetually fresh wonder and delight
wonder at the completeness and compactness of the synthesis, and delight at th
fresh and musical language, always as clear as a bell and as bright as the sky
through which her rays of lore come streaming in from all sides; wonder that so
little ever said has been left out, and pleasure at the natural and reasonable way
in which everything comes in, without effort or disturbance.

" Its place in all libraries is secured. It is a skillful exposition of the *Constant*
of the science, those facts which have been sifted and proved and quoted an
catalogued and made the basis of all modern argumentation upon the past. I
possesses a value that will not change, like that of other books written up for
sect or a side, and therefore incomplete, advancing the doubtful, because it i
needful for a theory, and suppressing the well known, because it is dangerous to
the theory. Mrs. Child's catholic sympathies with every genus and species of
human soul is certainly evident throughout her book. The true and tender way
she writes of every development of the genius of divine and human love show
how impossible it would be for her to limit it in a fixed and special theory, fo
that would necessitate fixed prejudices, for and on the other side, and therefore
gives the best possible guarantee, to the readers of her book, that she was also in
capable of garbling, overstating, suppressing the facts upon which many appa

rently opposite theories have been and must still be built up, the terms of none of which she might accept, but the spirit and light of all of which have already evidently mingled in her soul and governed with mild consistency the writing of her book. With this guarantee, its value will be felt by all true scholars, as a thesaurus of traditions and facts, many of them of difficult attainment, buried in volumes of high price, scarce and almost unreadable even in our best translations of them, but especially as an *arranged* exhibition of these, arranged, not arbitrarily, but on a natural system of easy reference.

"And we venture to predict that it will share the fine fate of those indispensable manuals, text books, encyclopedias, dictionaries, and synopses, which now make up the *working* libraries of students in every department of knowledge; of such a book, for instance, as the Cosmos of Humboldt, a book which in fact it more nearly resembles than any other written in modern times."—*Christian Register.*

"It shows great learning and great patience in the study and comparison of the ancient historians. Theologians and students may have known the facts brought forward in this work before, but Mrs. Child has arranged and ordered them in a way to make them plain and interesting to readers who have not had time or opportunity to go through so elaborate a course of study. The style is clear and good, and she has made a very interesting and instructive book. Young and old readers will find it well worth while to omit the reading of some of the alarmingly numerous novels, which all feel bound to keep the run of, in favour of a book which contains so much that they will find it good to read and remember."—*Boston Daily Advertiser.*

"We take up these volumes with feelings of gratitude and respect for the cherished authoress, which assure us of profit of some kind to be found in their perusal. The productions of her pen amused and instructed our boyhood, and we have ever since found food for heart and mind in her numerous, but none too numerous, works. Devoted, as her writings have always been, to the high service of truth and love, they have given her a deep place in the affections of her readers. In her present work, she has set before herself a task chosen with the utmost nobleness of motive, and pursued, of course, with candour and fidelity of effort. * * * * * Mrs. Child leads us through a survey of the world's religions, of those of them, we should say, which have sacred books, and endeavours to present to us their forms, their fundamental tenets, their development, and their spirit. India, Egypt, China, Thibet and Tartary, Chaldea, Persia, Greece, Rome, and the Celtic tribes, are thus challenged to give us a sketch of their faith, as an introduction to the religions whose records are contained in the Bible, and then the religion of Mahomet, brings up the close of the survey. We marvel alike at the industry of the writer and at the graces of simplicity and purity of style in which she has presented its results. Very valuable extracts from various 'sacred books,' as well as from our ecclesiastical stores, judiciously selected and admirably arranged, enable the reader to look behind his guide, and to judge of the fidelity of her course, while he is left to form his own conclusions, as hers are not obtruded upon him."—*Christian Examiner.*

"Every chapter has served to increase our sense of the vast amount of interesting information which the work contains, and to quicken anew our appreciation of the industry and research, the fearless truthfulness, the strict conscientiousness which must have presided over its preparation. 'The Progress of Religious Ideas' supplies a want which every one interested in the subject of which it treats must have felt. The facts are to be found indeed, but only after tedious research through many bulky volumes. In the English language, at least, there is no work which gives anything like so condensed, and yet so full a view of the ancient religions as this does."—*Christian Inquirer.*

"These are remarkable volumes. The history of various sects and of the Christian Church has been given, but we are not aware that any work has been before published in this country, having so large a scope as this. There are few writers, certainly few churchmen, who would have been capable of undertaking the task which Mrs. Child has well accomplished. To approach it required not merely high qualifications as a writer, a sound intellect, and unwearied research, but what most of those who might otherwise be competent to the task would lack, a freedom from scepticism on the one hand, and perfect religious toleration on the other. . . . . . But it is the facts which these volumes contain that will make them sought after."—*Boston Journal.*

A Guide to the Knowledge of Life,
Vegetable and Animal: Being a Comprehensive Manual of Physiology, viewed in relation to the maintenance of health. By Robert James Mann, M. D. Revised and corrected.

Extract from the Preface.

" In carrying out his plan of preparing a course of physiological instruction that shall be adapted equally to the wants of schools and of the public at large, the author has deemed it best to address himself *immediately* to the reason and intelligence of his readers. He has endeavored first to teach the broad principles upon which organization is based, and then to point out inferentially how these broad principles apply to sanitary regulations and considerations. The advantage of this proceeding over any more dogmatic handling of the subject, is that the student becomes trained by it to meet any new combinations of circumstances that may occur in life, with a fair chance of seeing their bearing correctly. He can apply broad principles in a thousand different ways, as unforeseen occasions arise. But particular and definite directions are liable in the ever-varying complications of social existence, to fail him at his greatest need. It is obviously the better course that the understanding should be possessed with the reason of things, and should be then left to make its own practical arrangements in accordance with its acquired insight, rather than that it should be told merely that this or that ought to be done. Accordingly, the "GUIDE TO THE KNOWLEDGE OF LIFE" treats of vitality in the broadest and most philosophic sense. The chemical and physical laws that are concerned with the work of organization, are first explained. The mutual relations and compensations of vegetable and animal structure are then indicated : and next the material composition of the several parts of the animated frame, and especially of the muscular and nervous apparatus, is sketched. After this, the constitution of the brain, and the connection of its substance with the faculties of instinct and intelligence, are dwelt upon mainly with a view of enforcing the great duties, and illustrating the capabilities of a sound course of education. Incidentally to these interesting topics, several considerations of the highest practical moment are entered upon : such, for instance, as the means by which the fresh air is made a hot-bed of pestilence ; the course whereby food is turned into poison, and drink into liquid venom ; and how sensual indulgence saps and destroys the vigor both of body and mind, whilst habits of self-control and refined intelligence develope in both the highest and noblest powers. Finally, the nature of disease, and the cause and meaning of premature decay, are viewed in relation to remedial and preventive measures. The "GUIDE TO THE KNOWLEDGE OF LIFE" is, therefore, a comprehensive statement of the fundamental principles of physiological and hygieinal science, fitted for the general reader and for educational use."

Books suitable for Presents and School Prizes,

PUBLISHED BY

C. S. FRANCIS AND COMPANY,

554 BROADWAY, NEW YORK.

A series of volumes, in prose and poetry, on fine paper, in various styles of handsome binding, and illustrated with fine engravings.

SIR WALTER SCOTT.

Poetical Works.

Complete. Best edition, with all the notes, prefaces, &c. In 6 vols. With illustrations.

Cloth, $4.50; half imitation morocco, $5.00; half calf, $8.00.

Poetical Works.

Complete in 2 vols. Illustrated with 8 steel plates.

Cloth, $2.50; cloth, extra gilt, $3.50; morocco, extra, $5.00.

The Lady of the Lake.

A Poem, in six Cantos. By Sir Walter Scott.

Marmion.

A Tale of Flodden Field. By Sir Walter Scott.

Lord of the Isles.

A Poem, in six Cantos. By Sir Walter Scott.

Lay of the Last Minstrel.

A Poem, in six Cantos. By Sir Walter Scott.

Rokeby.

A Poem. By Sir Walter Scott.

The above are from the author's latest editions, with his last correc tions, new introductions, and notes. Each in 1 vol. 12mo.

Cloth, plain, $0.63.	Cloth, gilt edges, $1.00.
Superfine edition, gilt, 1.25.	Morocco, extra, 2.25.

Waverley Poetry:

Being the Poems scattered through the Waverley Novels, attributed to anonymous sources, or presumed to be by Sir Walter Scott. With titles and index. Cloth, 75 cts.; cloth, extra gilt, $1.25.

"It will be found that this volume contains gems of rare beauty, many sparkles of wit, and many aphorisms of wisdom, which will serve for texts to innumerable lessons of morality, already or hereafter to be written."

THOMAS MOORE.

Lalla Rookh :

An Oriental Romance. A new edition, in one handsome volume with steel plate.

Cloth, $0.63. Fine edition, extra gilt, $1.25.
Cloth, gilt, 1.00. do. turkey mor., 2.25.

Irish Melodies and Sacred Songs.

From the last London edition of his collected works. 1 vol. 12mo.
Cloth, 63 cts.; extra gilt, $1.00; turkey morocco, $2.00

WORDSWORTH.

Poems of William Wordsworth ;

With an Introductory Essay on his Life and Writings, by H. T. Tuckerman. With a Portrait.
Cloth, 75 cts.; extra gilt, $1.00; morocco, $2.25.

The Excursion.

1 vol. 16mo. 75 cts.; extra gilt, $1.00; morocco, $2.25.

"The noblest poem in the English language since Milton's Paradise Lost."— *Dana.*

The Poems of Wordsworth ;

Including The Excursion, and a selection of his most characteristic and beautiful pieces. In one handsome volume.

COLERIDGE.

Poetical Works of S. T. Coleridge ;

With Introductory Essay on his Life and Writings, by H. T. Tuckerman. Complete in 1 vol. 16mo.
$1.00; extra gilt, $1.25; morocco, $2.25.

TALFOURD.

Tragedies, Sonnets, and Verses.

By Thomas Noon Talfourd. Containing Ion; The Athenian Captive; Glencoe; Sonnets; Verses.
Cloth, 63 cts.; extra gilt, $1.00; morocco, $1.75.

The only complete American edition of Talfourd's poetry.

"A most acceptable addition to the truly choice reading of the day."— *Knickerbocker.*

NORTON.

Poems of Mrs. Norton.

The Dream, Child of the Islands, and other Poems. By the Hon. Mrs. Norton. 1 vol. With portrait of the author.
Cloth, $1.00; extra, $1.50; morocco, $2.25.

iii·

MRS. HEMANS.

The Works of Felicia Hemans.

A complete and uniform edition, with a Memoir by her Sister, and an Essay by Mrs. Sigourney. In 7 vols. cabinet size, with Portrait. Price $4.00, in neat cloth, or on superfine paper, with illuminated titles ; $7.00, in half morocco, or calf. Also, the same edition, without the Memoir, in 3 vols., $3.00, cloth gilt, or $7.00 in morocco. Each volume may be had as a separate and complete book.

Price 62½ cents ; or in extra cloth, gilt edges, $1.00

Memoir of Mrs. Hemans.

By her Sister. With an Essay on her Genius, by Mrs. Sigourney.

Tales and Historic Scenes,

And other Poems. By Mrs. Hemans.

The Siege of Valencia,

The Skeptic, and other Poems. By Mrs. Hemans.

The Forest Sanctuary,

Lays of many Lands, and other Poems. By Mrs. Hemans.

Records of Woman,

Vespers of Palermo, and other Poems. By Mrs. Hemans.

Songs of the Affections,

National Lyrics, and other Poems. By Mrs. Hemans.

Songs and Lyrics,

Scenes and Hymns of Life, and other Poems. By Mrs. Hermans.

Each of the above, plain cloth, 62½ cts. ; extra cloth, gilt edges, with illuminated titles, $1.00.

MRS. BROWNING.

The Poems of Elizabeth Barrett Browning.

A new edition, carefully revised and corrected from the last London edition. 2 vols. 16mo.

Cloth, $2.00 ; extra gilt, $2.50 ; turkey morocco, $4.50.

Prometheus Bound,

Casa Guidi Windows, Sonnets from the Portuguese, &c. 1 vol. 16mo. Cloth, 75 cts. ; cloth, extra gilt, $1.25.

"I bow my head in reverence before the genius of the greatest English Poetess. Her last poem, 'Casa Guidi Windows,' has passages that Miriam might have sung to her timbrel over the sunken chariots of Egypt. The Portuguese Sonnets are among the most wonderful poems in any language. Their exquisite spiritual delicacy, their naturalness, their sincerity, and directness, place them in the highest rank."—*Lectures on English Poets, by Oliver Wendell Holmes.*

PUBLISHED BY C. S. FRANCIS & CO., NEW YORK.

Pycroft's Course of English Reading.

A Course of English Reading, adapted to every taste and capacity. By Rev. James Pycroft, of Trinity College, Oxford. Edited with alterations, emendations, and additions, by J. A. Spencer, D. D.

Extract from the Preface.

" Miss Jane C. divided her in-door hours into three parts: the housekeeping and dinner-ordering cares of life claimed one part; hearing two younger sisters say their lessons, a second part; and during the third, and most delightful remainder, she would lock her chamber door, and move on the marker of Russell's 'Modern Europe,' at the rate of never less than fifteen pages an hour, and sometimes more.

" Being so vexatious as to ask wherein her satisfaction consisted, I was told, it. the thought that she did her duty ; that she kept her resolution: that she read as much as her friends; that continually fewer histories remained to be read; and that she hoped one day to excel in literature.

" A few torturing questions elicited that neither the labor nor the resolution aforesaid, had produced any sensible increase, or more than a vague but anxious expectation, of available information or mental improvement. A painful suspicion arose that there was some truth in the annoying remark of a certain idle companion, that she was 'stupefying her brains for no good.'

" The exposure of an innocent delusion is mere cruelty, unless you replace the shadow by the substance; so, a list of books and plan of operations was promised by the next post. Adam Smith attempted in a pamphlet what resulted in his Wealth of Nations, after the labor of thirty years. My letter grew into a volume now offered for the guidance of youth in each and every department of literature.

" Without aspiring to direct the future studies of men, Macaulay in History, of Dr. Buckland in Geology, or of the Duke of Wellington in military tactics. he is happy to say, that very learned men have expressed their regret that in their early studies they had not the benefit of such simple guidance as this volume affords."

" A volume which we can conscientiously recommend as marking out an accurate course of historical and general reading, from which a vast acquisition of sound knowledge must result. The arrangement and system are no less admirable than the selection of authors pointed out for study."—*Literary Gazette.*

" An admirable little work, intended to suggest various ways in which the acquisition of knowledge through the medium of books, may be adapted to the leisure time and taste of those who would educate themselves. The plain terms in which the latter consideration is urged has something in them decidedly original; and especially would we commend Mr. Pycroft to the notice of those who feel at times overwhelmed by the heaped up piles of learning that beset the hesitating student."—*Albion.*

" We say unhesitatingly that this is a most excellent work, which should be in the hands of every student and reader of the English language; and we have to thank Dr. Spencer for the valuable additions he has made to it, admirably adapting it to American wants. Whoever will follow the advice it contains for one or two hours a day will soon acquire such habits of reflection, and so much general knowledge as will much increase the pleasure of both their solitary and social hours."—*Albany Spectator.*